A PARTRIDGE IN HIS FAMILY TREE

JOANNE AUSTEN BROWN

CONTENTS

Title: A Partridge in His Family (First Published in 2020 as part of the "12 Rogues of Christmas"—Republished as a Novella 2022)

Copyright © 2020 Joanne Austen Brown

BOOKS BY JOANNE AUSTEN BROWN

Always Louisa ~ Book One: Always Series

Always Elspeth ~ Book Two: Always Series

Rachael's Jaunt ~ Book One: Come with Me

Molly's Laird ~ Book Two: Come with Me

DEDICATION

To my wonderful editor, Nas, who has stood by me and encouraged me over the last three years to be the best I can be.

JASON DANIEL BAIRD

ondon 1818

"She is a little girl." Jason Daniel Baird was not happy. "Mother, she is not for me."

"Jason, she is the same age as you. You chose to be a rake. She chose to be pure. Not sweet and innocent but true to who she is. A Partridge, a member of one of the oldest families in London. At least she has breeding."

He continued to pace in front of the library window. He kept looking out the glass expecting the Partridge to jump out of the bushes.

"She hasn't married, Mother. She is twenty-eight. There must be something wrong with her. She probably despises men."

His mother stood and walked over to stand in front of him. She was angry. Her face was red, and her lips were tightly shut. She placed her hand gently on his chest. He almost flinched. He felt five years old again.

"Unlike you, son, she has carried the heritage of her family forward. Better than any man could. She replaced her father, as guardian of her mother and her niece. She is the head of a great family. She chose honour and tradition. If that is what is wrong with her, as you say, then give me more women such as her."

"So, I dishonour you, do I?" He stood taller and stared out the window. *He was an embarrassment.*

"No, my boy. I know that your raking days are over, but your reputation continues to follow you. I know you need to settle down and become ready to take the place of your father, when the time is right. She is a good match and you have known each other for many years."

He lowered his gaze to his feet. Take his father's place. Did he really want to be a lord of the manor and a lord in the house of parliament? He knew his father was not as well as he used to be. That his health had declined over the past few years.

He looked into his mother's deep blue eyes. And his breath stalled as he saw her strength and her forbearance shining through. He could be so stupid sometimes.

"Mother, I am sorry. I have not seen her in years, and I thought... Will you ask her for dinner? Or are we to meet at a ball?"

His mother wrapped her arms about him, and he took her into his arms. Now he wished he were five years old so he could sit on his mother's lap and forget the rest of the world.

"I am so proud of you, Jason. I will arrange a dinner. She doesn't usually attend many balls."

"Of course, she doesn't."

His mother looked into his eyes, and he grinned.

"I will behave."

She leaned up and kissed him on his cheek.

"Thank you, my boy. I don't think you will regret your decision."

His mother left the library with a definite bounce in her step. He shook his head. He was not sure this was a good idea. After all, Dianna Mariah Partridge was his first love and the reason, he became a rake.

She read over the missive again, dinner at the Baird's London home. Well, that was unexpected. Dare she say yes? She had hurt Jason all those years ago. But they were only children. Surely, he had forgotten all that childishness. Fourteen years of age and he was convinced they would marry. Then she had told him that he was nothing but a silly boy. He did not know what love was. Trouble was that over the years she had come to think he was right. No one filled that gap in her heart he had once held.

But he had become a well-known rake and love was forgotten. Especially by him. If she occasionally came back to her heart to see that empty space, she quickly closed the door, so it remained empty. Other men had tried to take his place, but they would never fit. Or could never fit. Life was simpler if that space remained vacant. Now she was given an opportunity to perhaps say sorry and see if they could be friends again. Or perhaps…

"What does it say, Diamond?"

She looked over to her mother sitting up straight in bed. "Diamond? You have not called me that in years. Why now?"

"It just seemed like you were a young girl again."

Her mother lowered her head. "You are still young. Sorry."

"No need to apologise, Mother. I felt like I was a fourteen-year-old again. So, you were right. That is where I was, being a young girl again."

"That's what I thought. Who is the letter from?"

"The Baird's. They are asking me to come for dinner at their home at Fitzroy Square. I will probably apologise…"

"Oh no… Don't do that. It will be lovely for you to see them all again. You were so close with Jason when you were younger. They say that he is a good catch, you know."

"Oh, really Mother, who says that? Your caldron of plotting friends? I have a lot of responsibilities now…"

"Which is why I would love to see you go. You have been so busy. It would be wonderful if you could relax for a time."

"But who will look after Ada?"

"Ada is fourteen years old so she can sit with me and the servants. After all it is only one night. And you deserve to enjoy yourself."

"It would be wonderful to see Lord and Lady Baird again."

"And Jason, of course. Don't forget him."

"I don't think you would let me forget him, Mother." Walking over, she gave her mother a hug. "I will go down and write a reply immediately. And yes, I will say yes."

She left the room on lighter feet. Her mother had colour returning to her cheeks. Even if it was at her expense.

She made her way down the staircase as Ada came bouncing up them.

"Can I go outside and visit the horses?"

"May I go and visit the horses?"

"Wonderful, we can go together."

"No, Ada. I was correcting your grammar. You may go but please do not get your lovely dress dirty. After I have finished some correspondence, I wish to go for a ride in Hyde Park and you may come with me if you like."

"Yippee," Ada squealed.

"Try to be lady-like please Ada. And put on your riding coat."

"I'm sorry, Aunt Dianna. I promise I will behave myself." She turned and ran down the stairs and out toward the back door and the mews.

Dianna watched her and chuckled. That girl would be the death of her. No, she should not think that way. She was a wonderful child. And Dianna was happy to be her guardian. But she would rather that her brother and sister-in-law were alive to watch her grow. Paul and Angela would be so very proud.

She continued to the study and sat behind her father's enormous desk. Except that it was her desk now. Father's estate was not entailed away to the next appropriate male. Some of the males in the family had tried and failed to take the job from her. She fought them all the way convincing all of society that she was not only capable but determined to achieve the goals that her father had set. And these last five years she had done just that.

Both their import and export textile company had done extremely well. She had learned at the feet of her father without him really knowing that she was learning. Until she was eighteen and begged to be more involved. She was surprised but delighted when her father agreed. A lord involved in working for a living and not just depending on his estate, her father was her source of strength. He believed in her and that was good enough for her.

She picked up the quill and started writing.

DEAR MRS BAIRD,

What a delight it was to receive your invitation to dinner on the 12th. Also, to know that you are currently in London. I would be delighted to attend your dinner and renew our friendship. I will arrive around 6pm as suggested.

Until then, Dianna Partridge.

* * *

THE SUN WAS SHINING between the clouds as Ada, and she made their way across the grass of the park. This could very well be one of the last fine days to ride. Being early in December, snow could be coming anytime soon. She pulled her coat closer as a shiver went through her. Even in the cold, Ada was flushed with the joy of riding.

"Ada dear, trot over to the trees at the left and then back and I will watch how well you keep your seat."

"Yes Aunt." And she trotted off.

"She looks very much like her father, Paul, does she not?"

Dianna turned to the voice. Jason. Her Jason. She stared into his beautiful deep blue eyes and another shiver shot through her. But this time it was not from the cold. This man was so handsome. His rustic brown hair curling on his collar. It was intolerable that any man should look so good. And his gaze lingered on her face for far too long.

"Jason." That was all she could say. Heavens, what a silly way to behave. She shook herself. "What a pleasure it is to see you again."

"Dear Dianna, the pleasure is all mine. How long has it been? Fourteen years, I believe," he said, answering his own question.

"Actually, it is nearly fifteen. Next month will be my brother and Angela's wedding anniversary. That was the last time we saw each other. At their wedding."

"Ah yes, you were a beautiful maid of honour to Angela, even though you were not of marriageable age. Only fourteen, were you not?"

"Yes Jason, I was, as you are well aware. Same age as Ada is now, who turned fourteen just a week ago."

"My, she is very young. Were we ever that young?"

"We were all that young once. But time has marched on."

He was staring at her again. Heat rose up her neck. She was going to blush. She turned to look at Ada. Her niece had turned at the trees and headed back toward her.

Jason's voice continued, "I would appreciate an introduction to your niece, being an old friend of your brother."

"I will but be warned, Jason, she will not be one of your conquests."

She looked at him as his smile vanished and his face reddened.

"I am sorry Dianna, that you would take my genuine interest in your niece as some kind of…"

"I am sorry, Jason. That was uncalled for. Please forgive me."

"I will but I will not stay to be introduced. I have errands to attend." He bowed his head to her and rode off.

She wanted to kick herself. She had been so cruel as to suggest that Jason would have a fancy for a child. Her heart ached. She had hurt him again. Ada approached her.

"Who was that aunt?" she asked with her sweetest voice.

"An old friend of mine and your father. I will introduce you next time we see him…"

* * *

Serves him right for wanting to be polite. She put him in his place almost immediately. Seems she has not forgotten what he had asked her all those years ago.

He had not even found out if she had received his mother's invitation to dinner.

She was more beautiful than he remembered, and he had thought of her many times over the years. Her chocolate brown hair and the pale blue eyes that captivated everyone she looked at. In her brown riding outfit and that silly red hat, she even looked like a Partridge. He chuckled to himself. A partridge looking like a partridge.

Her put down of him would not dissuade him. His mother was right. He still had deep feelings for her and wanted to make things right between them. He looked forward to the dinner. He turned to see her and her niece riding away in the other direction. He promised himself that soon he would hold that partridge in his arms.

* * *

WELL, *well, well.*

She had chased her old love off. Did that mean he might have a chance to woo her? A short laughter left his lips. He didn't want to woo her, he wanted to have his way with her. She was beautiful and everyone thought untouchable. That was an unspoken challenge he could not refuse. He would have her.

He turned his horse and rode after Baird. He needed to get some more information he knew the jilted lover could provide. He would and not even realise what he wanted the information for.

COMING RAKES

Usually, Jason enjoyed his club. But today he was not. Because today London's greatest rake, Henry Enfield was grilling him. He did not even want to admit he knew the man. But here he was, sitting on the lounge in front of him raving about his most recent conquests. He was growing tired of the conversation and was about to make his excuses to leave when he found himself frozen to his chair.

"I beg your pardon, who are you planning to seduce?"

"The lady who rejected you of course, Dianna Partridge."

"She did not reject me. We were children at the time. Hardly counts, I would think." He pushed down the nausea rising in his stomach. He would not allow this demon anywhere near her. "Surely she is too old for your usual conquests?" He didn't think Dianna was too old. She was older than most, but he saw her beauty so clearly this morning, and it was timeless.

"True, but a lady of wealth and prestige. Perhaps I should settle down?"

Jason wanted to wipe that smirk off the miserable man's face. He stood. "Just stay away from my friend, do you hear me?"

"Your friend? She and you did not seem very friendly this morning."

Trust the braggard to have been watching him or her for that matter.

"I am making you aware, that is all."

Now the beast stood and did not give him the pleasure of walking away but left him standing like a statue in front of his chair.

Jason sat back down. What should he do? What could he do?

* * *

"MOTHER, TELL ME YOU HAVEN'T?" He was pacing back and forth in front of the library window, again. This position was becoming a regular event.

"I have, my dear. Five of your rakish friends. I thought that would allow you to protect her from the rogues."

"But he has admitted to me that he plans to bed her."

She placed the book she had been reading on the chaise next to her. "My dear boy, she may not wish to bed him. In fact, she may not wish to bed anyone. But it will allow you to come to her rescue and keep all the men at bay. I do believe you will have your work cut out for you."

"You are so sure she will resist him?" He continued to pace.

"My dear, she is a woman of virtue. She will not place herself in a situation where she looks weak. She will put him aside. That will allow you to keep watch and she would be close to you."

"What if she wishes to put me aside? Then what?"

"For a rake, you ask some interesting questions. Let us just wait to see how things go, shall we?"

He nodded but was unconvinced.

"Trust me. I have seen the ton in all its glory. I have arranged things perfectly. Wait and see."

"Mother, why are you doing this? Is it really worth it?"

"Jason. I have watched you grow. I have seen you interact with many females. And only Dianna has been able to give to you as much as you dish out. She is well suited to you."

"So much for love?"

"On the contrary. Love can blossom from the very beginning."

"Somehow, I doubt it."

"Oh, yee of little faith."

He looked at his mother as she picked up the book and went back to her reading. The discussion would seem to have ended. He turned and left the library convinced that the whole dinner would be a disaster from which none of them would recover.

* * *

"WELL, I have accepted. Nothing more I can do now, despite my misgivings. Only three days to go and we will see what awaits me."

Walking over, Dianna sat at her mother's bedside. She had her doubts but was not going to worry her mother about the situation.

"Word has it, Lady Baird has invited other rogues to the dinner."

"Where on earth do you get your information, Mother?"

"My caldron of plotting friends." She smiled.

"Touché. What do your well-informed friends say will happen?"

"That you will be a great success. You are a woman who will not put up with these rogues. And Jason will beat all the gentlemen away so he can have you all to himself."

"You know I must come in and listen to your caldron the next time they visit. I might learn what they want me to do."

"No, no Dianna. We would not be so rude as to talk about you to your face." She started to laugh.

A little smile left Dianna's lips seeing her mother in such good spirits. She would be happy to see her joy remain.

"Well to keep your lovely caldron happy, I will spend most of my time with Jason. At least I have some knowledge of who he is even if he is a rake."

Her mother smiled and placed her hand on the pile of letters on her bed. "He is not a rake anymore. In fact, he has not been for some time."

Dianna shook her head.

"I am not going to ask, you know, so I will take your word for it."

"That would be advisable my dear." And her mother chuckled.

DINNER

The evening was already dark. Winter saw the darkness attack the city and plunge it into night by five. It was a mere ten minutes by carriage to the Baird's London house. Her hair was done, undergarments in place. All she had to do was place her dress and silk evening slippers on and she was ready to go. She put on her dressing gown and went to see how her mother was doing.

The candles were lit. She preferred them to the gas light.

"They are more romantic." Her mother declared as she came into the room. Ada was laying on the bed next to her with a book in her hand.

Both were looking at her attire.

"Are you going in your dressing gown, Auntie?" she sniggered.

"No, as you well know. I still can't decide which to wear—the blue or the red."

Ada looked at her. "You have pearls threaded through your hair. Either would look nice with them."

"But what impression does she want to give, Ada?"

Her mother sat straighter in bed.

"The blue will make her look regal, even untouchable, while the red will tell all that she is an independent woman who will wear what she wants."

"Are you challenging me, Mother?"

"On the contrary my dear, I believe you to be yourself and will chose what you want to wear."

"Then I will wear the red. Challenge accepted." Her mother was pleased, her smile not hiding the joy in her response.

"Then come and show us before you leave." Ada added.

She left the room and headed back to her bedroom. Red it was. Those rakes had better keep their distance. Red was a colour she loved.

Challenge accepted.

* * *

HER CARRIAGE HAD JUST PULLED up. She was politely late by only five minutes. All the rouges were here but he wanted to escort her in so was waiting in the library till she arrived. His mother was in the evening room entertaining the rakes. Something she had wanted to do, and he was happy to let her. She could keep them in their place.

He stepped into the foyer just as she came through the door. A bulky black travelling coat covered her almost head to foot. The butler helped her to take it off.

Bright red greeted his eyes. Red velvet in fact. She looked stunning. With her chocolate hair, the red made her glow. She turned to face him as he greeted her. Forget the red, scarlet was much more appropriate.

"Dianna, how wonderful you look. May I say that the pearls threaded through your hair gives you the appearance of a halo?"

"Ahh. Jason, what a delightful thing to say. But you know I am no angel."

"You might not be an angel, but you look angelic. Thank you for coming to dinner. My three female cousins are here also to make up the numbers. I believe you know them."

"Charlotte, Elizabeth and Victoria?"

"Correct."

"Yes, I have seen them from time to time."

"Well, let me escort you to the evening room. Can I have a sherry brought to you?"

"I will be delighted on both counts."

So far there was polite conversation between them, and he held his breath, just for a moment. He locked his hands together just for a second in the hope it would continue for the rest of the evening. He, then offered his arm and she gently placed her gloved hand onto it. A jolt of knowing shot through him. They looked at each other. She had felt it too. He smiled and was ecstatic to see a smile cross her face.

They entered the evening room and all conversation ceased. All eyes descended onto them as they came through the doorway.

"My dear Dianna." His mother made her way toward them. "I was delighted you accepted our invitation. I see Jason has already greeted you." She placed her hand on Dianna's shoulders and greeted her with a kiss on each cheek.

He saw her face redden. It was not from the reflection of her dress.

"Jason, my dear, please take Dianna around and introduce her."

A butler appeared by her side and offered her a sherry. She accepted it. He now walked her to where three men and two of his cousins awaited them.

"Miss Partridge, may I introduce you to Mr Henry Enfield, Sir Peter Bailey and the Honourable William Ashton. My cousins Charlotte and Victoria."

She curtsied to the gentlemen.

"So wonderful to see you again, Miss Partridge." Charlotte greeted her.

"Please call me Dianna."

Enfield smirked. "I hope we may all call you Dianna?"

Jason took in a quick breath. Dianna did not disappoint. "Perhaps by the end of the evening you might, but until then Miss Partridge will do."

There was no smile on his face now.

"Come Dianna, let me introduce you to the others."

He directed her to the other group of diners and introduced her around to everyone. He turned to look at Enfield who was not happy. He was red faced and frowning.

This evening was starting off well.

* * *

As THEY WALKED into the dining room, she smiled as Jason again offered his arm. He was most pleasant. Thanks to her mother, she had a fair idea about the new men she was introduced to. All seemed polite. But she was wary. All were known rakes.

However, she took an immediate dislike to Enfield. He was polite but had a slyness about him. A chill crept up her spine when she looked at him. His eyes held a craftiness which made her shiver.

Jason pulled out the chair into which she sat. Jason seated himself on her right and Sir Peter Bailey sat on her left. Unfortunately, Mr Enfield was seated opposite her. He had Victoria and Charlotte on either side of him. She hoped they would keep him occupied.

Lady Baird was at the right, at one end of the table. Jason had said his father was unwell and would not be joining them this evening, so the other end of the table was free. The other dinner guests were seated around them.

"I must say that the room is beautifully warm," Sir Peter said.

She turned to Sir Peter and replied, "Yes, but for a December evening I am pleased that it is."

"Very true. Do you ride, Miss Partridge?" he continued.

"I do, Sir Bailey."

"Oh, please Miss Partridge, call me Bailey. Most do. Don't often answer to Sir Bailey or even Peter."

"Then, will you please call me Dianna?" She made a point of looking at Enfield and saw his face grow red. She hoped he was put off. But he smiled at her, and she turned to look at Jason. Jason was glaring at Enfield. He then turned to look at her and a smile crossed his face.

"Are you still riding? The weather has been very cold," Jason asked.

"I have not ridden since the day I saw you. It has been very cold."

"What other interests do you have, Miss Partridge?" Enfield asked.

She looked across the table at Enfield. "Many things." She had no intention of revealing anything to him.

"Perhaps you would like to enlighten us? After all," he continued, "You are a great lady, are you not?"

"I am a lady, sir, but great, I would say not." But she could see he had no intention to let it stop there.

"But madam, are you not the head of the Partridge Clan now?"

"It is true that my father left all of his estate and businesses to me." She watched as the faces of the guests varied from looks of horror, surprise, and downright disgust. She looked at Jason prepared to condemn him, expecting the same reaction, but could see both pride and an air of protection around him.

She was both surprised and excited as he pushed back on his chair and stood.

"Ladies and gentlemen, would you please allow me to take Miss Partridge to the other room for a moment." He lifted his hand to the butler. The butler came over to the table and handed him a letter. "It would seem that a message arrived for Miss Partridge, and I would like her to read it in private."

His mother immediately took the lead. "Please take Miss Partridge into the library, my dear. We will go on with dinner and you can return when you are ready."

He offered her his arm and she stood. She was perplexed but was growing anxious believing that the note was urgent.

He escorted her out of the dining room and over the foyer to the library.

"Jason, what on earth is going on? Is the note from my mother?"

"I must apologise, Dianna. I got you out of the situation for my own reasons. I had arranged this note to be a way of getting you away from Enfield."

"That man is despicable. How dare he try to be so forward. He gives me the shivers and I'm not cold."

Jason escorted her to the chaise. She sat and he sat next to her.

"I brought you out as I wished to warn you. I will be blunt so please excuse me. In my club I heard him declare that he would try to make you his next conquest."

She stared at him and began to laugh. He looked perplexed even bewildered.

"He can declare all he wants but he will not succeed."

"I am not suggesting that he will. I wanted you to know so you could deal with him. Armed with the information, I hoped you would be able to forgive the fact that he is in our home. Mother had no idea."

"Do not be concerned, Jason. I do not blame you or your mother for his presence nor for the information. I am delighted that you have told me. I can be condescending now and not feel guilty."

"Please be careful. He has much power and I do not trust him. He has a demeanour to which I, too, get the 'shivers', as you say."

She placed her hand on his. "I take your warning seriously. I do not trust him, nor do I like him. I hear your warning. Thank you."

He stood and walked to the window. The curtain had not been drawn. He gazed out of the window a moment. He continued, "That is not the only reason I wanted to speak with you."

He turned and looked at her. "I wanted to say that I still admire you. And ask if I may spend more time with you. To renew the friendship that our families and dare I say we once had."

* * *

He looked at her face to see if he could determine her reaction. To him she seemed surprised but pleased. He continued looking at her, waiting for some indication. She again did not disappoint.

"I will admit to you that since I saw you in the park, I have been thinking on similar lines, so I am pleased to hear what you have said. We were always such good friends. And I would like to restart that friendship."

He came and sat on the chaise next to her. "I am delighted to hear it."

He put out his hand. "Shall we shake on it?" She looked down at his hand and gingerly placed her hand in his. "Then we have a deal. We are friends again." He did not let go of her hand.

"We are friends. Thank you for your concern and honesty."

He gave a deep long sigh. Things would now be better.

"Shall we return to dinner?" He stood; her hand held tightly in his. She stood and he placed her hand on his arm and they returned to the dining room.

MORNING GLORY

She lay in bed as the sun slowly rose. Her curtains were open. She adored waking to the light of a new day. And it really felt like something was different. The sun was shining brighter, the air was lighter and so were her spirits. She and Jason were friends.

The rest of the dinner the previous evening was a delight with her ignoring most of Enfield's snide comments. *She was always polite* but had great delight in putting the man in his place. Jason never left her side and always steered her toward his cousins who she believed had been warned to protect her from the rakes. Very few of them had the chance to speak to her as the ladies, Jason and even Lady Baird monopolised her time.

Jason had even escorted her to her carriage at the end of the evening, asking if he could call on her tomorrow. Today. Of course, she said yes. Now unlike her usual habit of rising for an early breakfast, she was lying in bed thinking of all the delights she had experienced the night before. The kiss he had placed upon her fingers and the warmth that radiated through her body.

The lingering fragrance of him hung in the air. They had been so near each other the night before, that his scent had permeated her senses and possibly her clothing.

After what felt like hours, and very enjoyable hours, she dressed and went to greet her mother. Ada was again keeping her company.

"You look well rested, my dear. How did the evening go?"

The heat rose from her neck and she smiled trying to distract from it.

"Auntie? Are you well? You look very flushed."

"I am fine, Ada. Thank you for your concern." She came and sat on the other side of the bed. She heard a little chuckle and gave Ada a serious look. The chuckle ceased.

"Well? Tell all." Her mother continued.

"Well, it was a lovely evening. Jason and I had a lovely time and his cousins, you know, Charlotte, Elizabeth and Victoria were all there."

"But what of the rakes? Did any of them impress you."

"No none. In fact, had Jason not been there the evening would have been a disaster."

"Ahh," added Ada, "the biggest rake of them all."

"I don't know what you mean."

"Well, everyone says that Jason has been a rake ever since..."

She saw her mother nudge the girl to stop her from talking.

"Mother, you know Jason has given up his rakish ways. I would rather Ada did not speculate about a gentleman she does not know."

"I'm sorry, Aunt," Ada jumped in. "Grandmama has not told me anything. I was quoting gossip, nothing else."

"Thank you, Ada, for your honesty. But please do not listen or involve yourself in any more gossip." She smiled at her niece and continued. "Jason is dropping in to see me this morning. We hope to see more of each other from now on."

The ladies were smiling but added no more.

She shook her head. "I'm sorry for sounding angry mama. I am not. I just want the friendship between the families renewed. And without speculation about him or me for that matter."

"Quite right, my dear. Now go and have your breakfast before the dear friend arrives."

She left the room shaking her head. She should not have said that to Ada. She promised herself to make it up to the girl, a smile touching her lips. Her mother did not believe the friendship explanation. And was sure that few others would either.

* * *

HE STOOD AT HER DOOR, hesitating. He was about to knock but was he too early? He knew that she would be busy with estate and family matters. But he could not wait. He wished to see her. He had lain awake half the night waiting to see her again. He knew that she was a more mature lady now. But she was still Dianna. And he was convinced that he still had deep feelings for her. Now he had to try and convince her that they should be together. Could she love him, again? She had once but never did admit it. He hoped she would soon.

He lifted his cane and tapped on the door. The Partridges' butler, who was ancient when he had seen him last, answered the door.

"Thomas?"

"Yes sir. How can I help you, sir?"

"Jason Baird to see Miss Partridge." He handed him his card.

"Yes, Master Baird, please come in and I will take you to Miss Dianna."

He stepped into the foyer. The black and white floor tiles making the room look quite large. As he waited for the old butler, he couldn't remember who had called him Master Baird the last time.

"Please follow me, sir."

And he did.

Old Thomas knocked on the study door and stepped in. "Master Baird to see you, ma'am." He stood aside and allowed Jason to step inside.

Dianna was sitting behind the desk and stood as he came into the room.

"Jason, what a pleasure. Please come and sit on the chaise. Thomas, can you bring us tea."

"Yes, ma'am." And he left the room.

Now, he was scared. Would she laugh at his silly idea? No. He did not think she would. So, he began.

"We had such fun last night. Thank you so much for coming. But I must admit I now have an ulterior motive for being here this morning." She looked so relaxed and so beautiful in the pale blue cotton dress.

She laughed. "We did have fun and much of it at Mr Enfield's expense."

They had given him a hard time of it. But he was not regretful.

"So, tell me your ulterior motive."

"I realised this morning that there are twelve days till Christmas."

"And...?"

"Well, I know that little rhyme applies to the twelve days after Christmas. So, I decided to change it." He placed his hand into the pocket of his jacket and pulled out an orange. He placed it into her hand.

"An orange?"

"I believe a very welcomed gift in the Netherlands. I plan to give you a small gift over the next twelve days. Small things and we can spend the time when we meet, getting to know each other again."

"Oh Jason, what a lovely idea. Meet every day from now until Christmas. Will you allow me to join in? In the gift giving side?"

"I had not thought about it. But why not? It must be a small gift. Something that reminds you of me and vice versa."

At that moment, the tea arrived.

"I had asked cook to bake you your favourite biscuit. Ginger Butter biscuits."

"Why, you have got the idea already before I had even explained it. Thank you. That is my favourite biscuit still."

"Then why an orange for me?"

"That is a little more complicated. I wanted to give you something that reminded me of you. These oranges that grow in our town greenhouse are so sweet. But occasionally they are unexpectedly sour."

She looked shocked.

"Don't misunderstand me, you are sweet, but you can be sour when you need to be, and I appreciate that. The way in which you protected yourself from Enfield brought a big smile to my face. I was proud of you."

She beamed at him, and warmth filled him. He had made her happy, so she looked happy. And he had been honest with her. He took her hand and placed the orange in it and his breath caught. This idea would keep them meeting till Christmas.

* * *

She loved his idea and he seemed to like her strength of character. Instead of fearing her 'sour' side, he looked like he was proud of her.

His idea of small gifts was also good, and she must sit down and make a list of small gifts she could get him. The fact he even accepted she too wished to do the same, gave her a great deal of encouragement.

She poured him a cup of tea. "Black and no sugar if I remember."

He smiled. "You remember correctly. I know you had not planned on the biscuits as a gift, but I am happy to accept them. Now tell me why and what they remind you of, in relation to me."

"I know you loved ginger. So, I wanted to give you something that would please you and I guess, would show you I remembered after all these years."

"And they have. Thank you. And I will ask your cook if I can take some home to Mother, who also loves ginger."

"Most definitely."

There was a knock at the door and the butler came in.

"Excuse me ma'am, there is a gentleman at the door. A Mr. H Enfield."

He was reading from a calling card in his hand.

"Please tell Mr Enfield that I am not at liberty to see him."

The butler closed the door.

"The man has persistence if nothing else." Jason commented.

She looked at him and he seemed both angry and concerned. He looked at her and the side of his mouth lifted but the look was more a grimace than a smile.

"Please. I know that I have no right to tell you who you can or cannot see. But I truly dislike the man and hope you will not see him. I beg of you, Dianna."

"My dear friend," yes, at that moment he was dear to her. "Do not fret, I have no desire to see the man ever again."

He took her hand and lifted it to his mouth and placed a gentle kiss on her fingers. Butterflies invaded her being. They fluttered around in every space inside her body. She smiled. It was good he was here and heard her openly reject Enfield's advances.

"Now, let us have our tea and I will tell you what I have planned for tomorrow," he added.

GUNTER'S

The next day he called for her at the same time and took her on a carriage ride. He wanted to keep the destination a surprise. The carriage was closed, and he had hot bricks wrapped and placed on the carriage floor to keep their feet warm. And beautiful fur rugs to wrap around them. She did not even have to bring a travelling coat.

As they pulled up at 7 Berkeley Square, she immediately recognised Gunter's Confectionery shop.

"It is a little cool for the ices," she said, not wishing to sound rude.

"So very true. But they serve tea, do they not?"

"They do indeed, and I could think of nothing nicer."

He escorted her down the carriage steps and straight into the shop. One of the attendants took them to a table near the fireplace. There, she was served with tea and plates full of sweetmeats, sugar plums, marshmallow, fruits both fresh and dry. And a vast assortment of biscuits and pastries.

He enjoyed the pleasures and chatted heartily about times when they had been children and what fun they had had.

"Do you remember the day we ate all those glorious plums at Farmer Millers? And we were so terribly ill?"

"I could hardly forget. We got in so much trouble and had to pick the remainder of the crop for him, but not allowed to eat one."

He laughed out loud. "I didn't look at a plum for years after that."

"What a delight this has been, Jason. But it is somewhat extravagant."

"Perhaps, but how else do we enjoy such beautiful sweets other than going personally to Gunter's?"

"Why sweet meats?"

"All of the vast assortments of treats remind me that you are more than what you seem. You are a woman of taste. But you are also intelligent, resourceful, strong and a great organiser."

She again could feel the heat rising to her face.

"I think you spoil me."

"Most definitely. What are friends for?"

"But I think that you are trying to convince me that I am more when perhaps I am not. After all you organised this," she waved her hands to the various beautiful treats. "I did not."

"It is true but when I thought of sweets, Gunter's was all I could think of. I lack imagination. Forgive me."

"Do not seek forgiveness. I forgive nothing. This has been a delight."

A small basket was brought to the table and any of the items they had not completed were placed in the basket. But there were more treats in the basket as well. The basket was then handed to her.

"For you to take home to your mother and niece. And you can share the sweetness."

"Thank you. They will love them. My gift seems somewhat small and insignificant."

"Before you give it to me, tell me why this gift."

She reached for her reticule and placed her hand inside. "The fragrance always reminds me of you. Wherever I am if I smell this scent, I have thought of you. It has happened over the years. I always think of you." She pulled out a small brown paper package and handed it to him.

His face was solemn as he unwrapped it. Within the brown wrap was a bottle of sandalwood oil.

"This also is hardly a simple gift. I adore it. Thank you." He took her hand and held it. "It warms me to know that this fragrance has reminded you of me over the years. Thank you again."

"Well, what have we here. A lover's tryst?"

* * *

JASON LOOKED up into the face of Enfield. He closed his eyes wanting to smack the man's face to the other side of the room. He gave Dianna's hand a little squeeze. Suddenly her hand was gone.

"You, sir, are not welcome here." he heard her say. Opening his eyes, he saw she was standing in front of Enfield, threatening him with her stern looks. She had pluck, but he feared it would get her into trouble when it came to Enfield.

He stood and placed himself between Enfield and Dianna. "Shall we go, Dianna? Fetch our carriage please." he said to the waiter.

"Yes, lets. The weather has changed so suddenly." She grabbed her basket and reticule and headed for the door.

He grabbed his gift and was about to follow when Enfield got in front of him.

"Trying to bed her yourself, are you?"

He again closed his eyes holding on to his temper as best he could. "I suggest you get out of my way, or you will find yourself on the ground." He went past him and left him standing there. The ghastly man had not replied, and he knew that did not bode well. The man was a reprobate.

* * *

"I will not let that stupid man spoil what a beautiful morning we had. Thank you, Jason. Shall we meet again tomorrow? Allow me to pick you up this time."

She wanted him to get his mind off Enfield. She could see that he was very angry. His face was red, and he said little on the short ride back to her home.

"I am sorry, Dianna. Yes, I will await you at my home tomorrow."

She placed her hand into his. "I really did have a wonderful time."

"I did also. And thank you for my sandalwood. I will cherish it."

She got out of the carriage and made her way to the door. She turned to wave goodbye as the carriage headed off. He was frowning and she was sure he was disappointed, and she did not blame him. That Enfield was abhorrent.

* * *

He wanted to cry out. Scream. Enfield was right, he did want to bed her. But what that evil man did not realise was he wanted her in his bed forever. As his wife. And now he was more determined than ever to protect her, despite her being very capable of protecting herself.

JDB

Day three of their gifts for each other was a day in which she could give back to Jason. His idea had been a wonderful diversion and she wanted to make the most of it. Today, she had arranged a place that hideous man Enfield could not ruin with his presence. She sent her carriage to pick Jason up at the usual time. He was then brought to the house. He, her mother, and Ada were brought to the study and tea was waiting for them when he arrived.

"What a wonderful surprise. I get to have tea with three of the most beautiful women in London."

He certainly was in better spirits than yesterday, but could it be all a pretence? She wanted him to be distracted before her real surprise.

"This is Ada. Ada this is the Honourable Jason Baird. He is a very good friend of mine and was of your father also."

Ada curtsied and Jason bowed to her.

He took her hand. Bowed again, "I am delighted to meet you, Ada. I had said to your aunt that I believe you looked a lot like your

30

father but now that I see you up close, I can see that you are a perfect blend of both your mother and father."

Ada beamed and curtsied again. She ran to the chaise to sit at her grandmother's feet. Her mother was still resting with her feet up on the chaise.

Jason came over to her mother and bowed. "A delight to see you again, Lady Partridge." He took her hand and kissed her fingertips.

"Delighted to see you again, my boy. Sorry, I cannot greet you in the standing position."

"No need to apologise madam, your daughter has explained, and I only can hope and wish that you will recover as soon as you can."

"Thank you, my dear. Now please sit down as Dianna gives you your tea."

They had delightful few hours together and shared a light luncheon. Her mother was taken back to her room to rest, and Ada went to have some classes with her tutor. She was a wonderful scholar, just as Dianna had been at that age. Finally, she was alone with Jason.

"Your mother is such a wonderful lady. I do hope her health improves. Your gift of tea with them was refreshing. Thank you."

"They were my light entertainment but not my gift. Come with me."

Jason followed her out into the mews behind the house and into the stables.

"I wished to give you the gift in the right environment and also in a place where we could not be disturbed by a certain gentleman."

He seemed perplexed. She walked over to a hay bail on which sat a long gift, wrapped in brown paper. She picked it up and handed it to him. Slowly he unwrapped it, looking at her often.

* * *

"IT IS MAGNIFICENT." There in his hand was a beautifully leather crafted riding crop. He turned it over and over, looking at it from all angles.

"So intricate."

"My stable master makes items in leather for the whole estate. He had this so I asked him to personalise it for you." She pointed to the end flap that had his initials burnt into the leather. JDB.

"You remember my middle name?"

"Yes. Isn't that what we are about? Remembering things that we know about each other. Jason Daniel Baird."

He wanted to take her into his arms and kiss her senseless. He stared into her glorious blue eyes. Such a thoughtful gift.

She leaned in.

"I hope you like it."

He leaned in closer to her. And whispered, "I am moved. I adore it and…"

"Yes?"

"And you." He lifted his hand to touch her cheek. "Thank you."

He closed his eyes and gently kissed her pink lips. Smooth, warm, and soft they were. And he had never experienced such ecstasy before.

She leaned into him, placing her arms around him. He placed his hand from her cheek to the back of her soft and delicate head. He deepened the kiss. Time stood still as they opened their mouths and explored each other.

Not because he wanted to but because if he did not, he would take her here and now on the hay, he stopped the kiss.

He leaned his head on her forehead. "Dianna, I hope you are not troubled by this kiss?"

"No. It is something that I have longed for. I hope you do not mind?"

"Mind?" God, he had been wanting this all his life. He hoped she did too.

"No, I do not mind. Dianna, this has only confirmed for me…"

"That you still love me?"

"Yes. I love you, my wonderful Dianna."

He kissed her gently on the lips again.

"I think that I love you."

"Only think?"

"I want to be sure."

"I will do whatever you want to convince you not only of my love but that you love me also."

He held her close. She snuggled into the embrace, her head resting on his chest. "Your heart and mine are beating in time."

"And I would like that to be forever. But I do not want to rush you."

"What on earth do you mean?" She pulled away from him.

"I want to marry you, Dianna."

"I thought you wanted to bed me?"

"I do but in the purest of motives. I want you to be my wife."

She walked a few steps away. Crossed her arms and looked at him.

"Am I not suitable affair material?"

He looked at her and shook his head. Didn't she understand that he wanted her to be his wife?

"Other men think that they would like to bed me."

"Other men see you as a cause not a partner. They want another notch on their bed post."

"So, you are saying I'm not attractive enough?"

He sat down on the bale of hay, shaking and ill to his stomach with what he was hearing. He ran his hand through his hair. He was still holding the whip. He balanced it in his hands. Turned it over and over. How on earth did he get here? Kissing the love of his life and her not believing it.

"You are the most beautiful woman of my acquaintance. I wish I were still the rake, who could throw you in the hay and make mad and passionate love to you. Believe me. I want to, more than you know. But I want your friendship and your love. I want all the things I have dreamed of and that I have only ever wanted with you."

She was kneeling in front of him. "I am sorry if I seemed cross. I wanted to hear that you were serious. I am sorry. We have a simple matter to complete."

"What do you mean?"

"We will continue with the gift giving and on the night of the last gift, you will ask me again, about marriage, and I will give you, my answer."

He stood and took her in his arms and gave her another passionate kiss. He again rested his head on her forehead. "You have a deal, my lady. But please do not scare me like that again. Come, take me inside and I will give you the gift I brought." He took her by the hand, and they walked back inside.

Back in her study he picked up the package that he had brought with him. They sat together on the chaise as she opened it.

She held the book in her hand. "A copy of *Shakespeare's Love Sonnets*."

"Yes. A first edition from my estate library. It is yours."

"But this would cost you a great deal."

"Actually, I hope that you can one day bring it back to my library, as my wife."

"You really are serious?"

"Yes, I am, and I hope that one day you will see that. For now, I will depart, and I will pick you up tomorrow, again at our usual time."

"Eleven o'clock." They said in unison.

"Until then." He bowed, then leaned over and kissed her gently on her cheek.

ELEVEN O'CLOCK

$\mathcal{A}$s eleven struck on the clock in the foyer, Dianna was waiting, ready to leave when Jason arrived. As she expected he was on time. They went for a ride in his carriage, but to no place in particular. This delighted her. They rode all over town. In the carriage it was private and warm. Under the beautiful furs she held his hands. She listened to his stories of life away from her and she shared her experiences too. This was private and wonderful.

"Father was always instructive. He considered me a woman of intelligence."

"Well. You are. But I know what you mean. Even my three cousins are not given the honour they deserve. They, too, are very intelligent."

"They are indeed. Chatting with them at dinner the other evening I could see that in them. But what of you? Did you just continue to be a rake?" She squeezed his hand and he squeezed it back.

"I was so angry with you when you told me that I was being

childish. Of course, I was, a child but you can't tell a boy who thinks he is a man that he is not."

"So, when I went to school at Oxford, I started the life of a rake and thought that I loved it. At first it dulled the pain of not having a piece of your heart anymore."

She placed her head on his shoulder. "I am sorry."

"No, you were right. I was not mature enough to think straight. Then four years ago my father became ill. I went back to my studies and committed myself to learning all that I could so that I could make him happy. I believe he was very proud of what I have done."

"I am sure he is."

He replied. "But he doesn't say, so I can only hope."

"Men find it hard to tell their children they are proud, unless they have a daughter who is relentless as I am."

He looked deeply into her eyes. She loved his eyes because she could see his truth. What he believed in, what he really wanted.

"I wish I could be more like you." He sighed deeply and leaned his head back into the seat of the coach.

"Thank you, my love, for sharing that with me."

He closed his eyes. "You are most welcome."

She put her head on his shoulder again and snuggled into his warm body. She was excited at how much love has blossomed between them since the dinner party.

* * *

HE HAD ARRANGED that they stopped at the Star & Garter Inn at Pall Mall. Maybe they could continue their discussions and have a bite to eat. The landlady took them to a private room where a beautiful fire was lit, and the room was warm.

They ate bread and cheese and had red wine to drink. Then a serving of roast duck and potatoes, followed by more bread with beautiful honey and homemade preserves.

On their way back to the carriage who should be in the court-yard but the dreaded Mr Enfield. He bowed to them both and walked into the inn. Dianna chose to ignore him.

She noticed that Jason was snarling at his back, as the idiotic man entered the inn.

"Well, at least he did not get the chance to spoil our meal," she added.

"True, but I am concerned that he seems to appear whenever we are out in public. It is as if he is following our every move."

They got into the carriage and placed the furs around them.

"I have my gift that I would like to give it to you on our trip back home," she added.

"Yes, but please allow me to go first. You have changed in many ways, all of which are wonderful, but there is one thing that when I take in a deep breath, I can only ever think of you." He handed her a package which she duly unwrapped.

It was a beautiful bottle. It contained her most favourite perfume. Jasmine.

"Jasmine is you. Everything about its subtle smell conjures pictures of you in my mind. Please accept this gift with my love firmly attached."

"My, my, Mr Baird, you are becoming quite the poet. Thank you, my dear." She opened the bottle and dabbed a little behind her ear. He closed his eyes and took a deep breath in, and sighed, revealing a smile of contentment on his face.

"I am sorry that I stole your idea. Actually, it was on my list before you gave me the sandalwood."

"It will be interesting to see what we have planned for each other, for I have made a list also."

He chuckled.

"Now, it is your turn. I have been working on it for a few days. I finished it last night and one of my servant's framed it overnight so that I could give it to you today." She handed him a small package which he calmly opened. He drew in his breath.

"You made this?"

"I know many people think that I am not the type of person who has the skills most women have. But I love to embroider. Hence, your initials have appeared yet again.'

She had done the J in a beautiful purple and the D in a different shade of purple. The B was gold thread. And all three letters were boarded in black thread. The material onto which it had been embroidered was a piece of the old Baird tartan of blue, green, and black stripes with a thin line of crimson purple.

"It is beautiful," he said in a whisper. "I had no idea you could embroider. It is a delight. I will have it beside my bed always. That way I can wake each morning looking at it and think of you."

He moved closer to her and kissed her delicately on her nose. "I love it."

She returned with a kiss on his lips.

The trip to her home was not long enough. Before long he was escorting her to the door. He bowed. Kissed her fingers and promised to see her tomorrow at their usual time.

INDEPENDENCE

That evening after dinner, Diana was sitting with her mother in her room.

"He adored it, Mother. He was honestly moved by such a small token."

"It really isn't such a small token. You created something about him and just for him. It was a beautiful idea, and I am very proud of you."

"Thank you, Mother. Mother, I think I have fallen in love with him."

"I would think that you have," she said with ease. "I think you are both very much in love."

"But we barely know each other?"

"On the contrary, my dear daughter. The two of you have known each other all your lives. I will admit you have not seen a lot of each other in the last few years but in these few days all has been renewed. You have shared more of those missing years with each other than many others would have. And I believe that is because you know each other still."

Dianna sat there looking at her mother and wondering why she had never noticed the wisdom coming from her thoughts. She was blessed to have a mother who knew her so well.

"Can I marry him and still have the independence that I have fought so hard to obtain? And will he tire of me and return to his rakish ways?"

"If he truly loves you, you already have it, your independence. Test the waters and see what he thinks. You and he could go to the estate in Kent and see what he thinks of all the changes you have made in both the estate and the business? Trust him. You may discover a partner rather than an accuser or a rake."

"Mother, you amaze me and yes you are right. I will talk with him tomorrow."

Dianna looked down at the book in her hand. She was not reading it, not really. She was using it to allow her time to think. She lifted it and pretended to read. Her mind was totally occupied by Jason.

* * *

HE SAT with his mother on the chaise in the library. His mother had taken off her slippers and was resting her feet in his lap. He had a book in his hand, but his thoughts were with his Dianna. His Dianna, how good that sounded.

"Mother, may I ask you a question?"

"Of course, my dear. What is it?"

"Do you think I am capable of loving anyone? I mean, I was a rake. Something that I am not proud of. But can I truly love?"

She took the book from his hands and placed it on the chaise.

"Yes."

"That is all? Just yes."

"Mr dear boy. Actually, I need to stop calling you my dear boy. Because you are not a boy anymore. Forgive me."

"Mother?"

"Jason, you love her, and she loves you."

"But we barely know each other."

"Nonsense. You grew up knowing each other. I admit you have not seen much of each other in the last few years, but you are both still the same. Has she changed much?"

"No. She is still Dianna."

"Then you have answered your own question. Did you love her then?"

"You know I did."

"Then I would say that you love her now."

"Yes Mother. I do."

"Then these days you have given to get to know her again, will confirm that love."

"I think they may have proven that already. I love her. I do not doubt it. Thank you, Mother."

"No need to thank me. You knew what you were feeling." She picked up the book and gave it back to him. She leaned back into the chaise and closed her eyes. Her face showed her contentment. And he could feel his.

He put down the book. Trying to read it was pretence. All he wanted to do was think of Dianna. Closing his eyes, he pictured her in his mind. And a smile lit his face.

WESTMINSTER

It was Sunday. They had arranged to meet at an earlier time. Usually, Dianna attended the little St Marys church not far from her London home. But he asked if they could attend the service at Westminster. And she had agreed. Ada would also attend.

He was now waiting at the front portico for her arrival. He loved this old cathedral and was wondering if they should marry here.

Enfield was coming through the main doors. What on earth was he doing here? The man was heading straight for him.

"What a surprise to see you here, old man." He bowed to him.

He returned the bow but was not interested in the greeting. He could see Ada and Dianna coming through the door, He bowed again at Enfield and headed toward them.

"That Enfield is here." He bowed to them both.

"Bully for him. I do not care. Let us ignore him and find a place to sit."

He made his way behind them up the Nave and as close to the choir as they could get. They all found seats. Ada sat first, then

Dianna and finally he. He wanted to be in isle seat to prevent the approach of Enfield should he dare to come near them. He turned to see where Enfield was and was pleased to see that he was sitting some rows back and looking seriously uncomfortable. Serves him right. He doubted the man had stepped into any church in years. He turned to face forward and tried to put his mind toward the day they would spend together and not about that odious man.

Dianna touched his arm and he looked down into her eyes and smiled.

"Forget him. This is a beautiful day and a beautiful church. Let us think about the day and not that silly man."

"I shall, my dear. Thank you for the reminder. While we await the service to begin, I would like to give you, my gift. May I?"

"Of course. But I must tell you that I cannot give you mine till after luncheon. Can you wait?"

"I can and will look forward to it." He heard Ada's giggle and looked over to her and smiled. He handed Dianna the small brown wrapped parcel and waited as she patiently unwrapped it.

"Oh, a beautiful prayer book. Thank you so much, Jason. It is a very thoughtful gift. As you can see my current book is well worn and your gift is timely."

"Not at all. I know you love to attend service and thought a new one might not go astray."

"May I look?" asked Ada.

"Of course, you may."

"It is beautifully made, Aunt, and has a lovely leather cover." She breathed in the intoxicating aroma and sighed. "I love new books."

* * *

THE SERVICE BEGAN and lasted for about an hour. Every now and then she noticed Jason searching for Enfield but by the end of the service he was more relaxed as Enfield had gone.

They rode in her carriage back to her home where they had luncheon. It was here that her mother started the ball rolling, as she called it.

"Dear Jason, I have a request to make of you."

"By all means ma'am, I am at your service." He bowed to her mother.

"I wondered if you would accompany us to the estate so that we can prepare for Christmas. I have an invitation here for your family to come and join us at Greenwood House, closer to Christmas and for the day itself." She passed the invitation to him which he placed into the inside pocked of his dress coat.

"I will be delighted and will have my mama respond to your invitation as soon as she can. When would you like to depart.?"

"I understand the weather will be agreeable tomorrow and as we are just three hours away by carriage, I suggest that we leave after luncheon tomorrow."

"I am agreeable."

He smiled at Dianna who was grinning with delight.

Her mother continued. "I must say that I have an ulterior motive." Dianna's face paled as she turned to look at her mother with dismay.

"I want to see if you can support my daughter to be the great woman she is. And that I wish for her to always be."

Dianna lowered her gaze as heat made its way up her neck and to her face. He reached his hand over to hers, resting in her lap and gave it a squeeze. She looked into his eyes, and he smiled.

"Madam, I have every intention to see Dianna be who she was born to be."

All three women were smiling, and he was delighted. Everything was going to plan. By Christmas he would propose to his Dianna. Now that they would leave London, they could rid themselves of Enfield and his plot to have her. Life was very good, but did he deserve it?

* * *

Ada stood and went to the piano. She sat behind it and patiently waited for her aunt.

"This is my gift to you, Jason." She stood and came to stand near Ada.

"I'll have you know, my boy, that this is a most singular talent that she has, and she does not share it often."

He sat up and placed his teacup on the table. And she began.

Ada played an introduction and then golden notes came from Dianna's lips. Her voice was sweet, and she sang beautifully. Notes that rose and descended and she captured him with each utterance.

As she finished, he stood. She came to him.

"That is today's gift to you. I hope it is acceptable."

"More than acceptable, Dianna. I want to hear that melody again and again for the rest of my days." He looked around just in time to see her mother and Ada leave the room.

"Your mother walked out. She must be feeling better." He chuckled. He took her in his arms, and they kissed. A kiss that was sweet and provided him with a longing that could not be forgotten.

He rested his head on her forehead. "I could kiss your mouth forever."

"Jason, I am sorry that my mother was so forward."

"Don't be, my dear. I want you to continue with your family duties. I just ask that I can be a part of it. Share the load. But only if you want to."

"I do want you to help. Some of my ideas can be tried on your family estates when the time is right."

"Then these days leading to Christmas will be a chance for you to show me what you can do and what you can teach me."

He kissed her again. But he soon pulled away from her. This was so hard. He wanted her kisses more than anything, but he was sure he could not stop if he didn't stop now.

"I will depart now, my dear. I have some serious packing to do. I will have my goods sent to Greenwood separately and will come here to accompany you all in the carriage to your home." He reluctantly pulled himself away, bowed, and left the house.

* * *

Enfield watched him leave. The man was gaining too much headway with the chit. He would have to rid himself of the gentleman so that he had a chance. He watched him get on his horse and trot away. Now, he had to work out what to do. He left his man to stay and watch the movements of the morning. He headed for home. Another night alone.

OFF TO KENT

Jason was excited at the gifts that awaited his Dianna. He had loaded them into his carriage, and they had departed for Kent some hours ago. He got atop his horse and rode to Dianna's house. He kept looking around but saw no sign of Enfield anywhere. Perhaps the missive he sent to him last night, warning him off had done the trick. He might have given up at last.

The Partridge carriage was out front when he arrived. The driver seated on top. He handed the reins of his horse to the servant that approached him, who took his horse to the rear of the carriage and tied it to the rear bar. He had his gift for Dianna and placed it in the carriage.

Dianna came down the steps, dressed in her travelling coat. He really did not like that coat as it covered her completely. And he loved to admire her beautiful shape.

Lady Partridge was helped down the stairs by two servants. Dianna approached him.

"We are ready if you are, Jason."

"My dear," he bowed. "I am ready."

Ada came running down the stairs toward them. "Aunty, the cart with all our luggage left about an hour ago."

"Thank you, Ada. Now go and sit with your grandma." The girl dutifully went and sat with her grandma in the carriage.

"Is all ready?" he asked her in a whisper. "Yes, my dear, though I did want to tell you, that the servants noticed a man watching the house for the last day."

"Man, what man?" He looked this way and that.

She placed her hand into his. "Not Enfield. But it could have been a servant. My coach man told him to leave, and he did."

"I will ride my horse and keep guard if you would prefer?"

"No need. I just wanted you to know. But please ride with us in the carriage. I would rather you with us."

This news of the strange man disturbed him greatly. Surely this man would not attempt any silly accident.

"Let me help you into the carriage, my love. I wish to have a chat with your coachman." He escorted her into carriage and then went to talk to the driver.

"If you see the man you told to leave anywhere, between here and Kent, I wish to know. Do you understand?"

"Yes sir."

"I am concerned for the family. Please keep a keen eye."

"I will, sir."

He hopped into the carriage, and they started out.

* * *

DIANNA COULD SEE that he was watchful through the whole trip. She doubted herself for a moment. Should she have told him? But he would want to know, and she did not want to keep things from him.

The trip had been uneventful, but she breathed a sigh of relief as the carriage stopped in front of Greenwood House. Everyone was glad to have arrived.

Servants appeared and helped Lady Partridge into the house.

"Diamond, Ada and I will rest in my room and have afternoon tea. You and Jason relax, and we will see you at supper." She made her way slowly up the steps.

"You know, I had quite forgotten that your pet name was Diamond."

"Mother has just started calling me that name again. It was due to my daydreaming. She said I looked like I was a small girl again."

"You are beautiful as a diamond. I must commend her on her wise decision to start using it again." He took her in his arms and hugged her.

"I believe you might be jesting with me, sir." She chuckled.

"Not at all." He placed a gentle kiss on her lips. "I will meet you in the library in half an hour. I wish to talk with the coachman and then get my gift for you."

She reached up and gave a light kiss on his lips in return. "Very well, my dear."

He turned and headed to the rear of the house and the stables. She was relieved that he was himself again. She watched him turn the corner and then she went indoors.

He watched from the crop of trees near the entrance of Greenwood. His servant had done well to find out they had headed here. Now, he needed to watch and wait for the right moment when he could make his move. As for the letter from Baird, he was not scared off. He pulled the missive out of his coat pocket and tore it up, throwing the pieces to the ground. He wanted her as his next conquest, and he always got what he wanted.

I LOVE GREEN

He made his way to the library. He had not been in the house for many years but remembered it as if he had been walking the floor but yesterday. He had the box, which he had retrieved from the coach, with her gift in one hand, he tapped on the library door with the other.

He heard Dianna's voice. "Enter."

"Oh Jason, you do not need to knock." She came over and gave him a hug. "I want you to feel like this house is your own home."

"But I may have found you in a compromising position." He chuckled. "A gentleman always knocks."

She gave him another hug. She was warm and soft. She had changed into a beautiful pale green day dress. A soft woollen shawl was draped over her shoulders. All her clothes were of the finest quality. He knew his gift for her would be perfect with the outfit she was wearing.

He handed her the box. A square and large box that gave no clue to its contents. She walked to the chaise and sat down, and he followed her over. There where he wanted to sit was another box, about the same size as the one he had just given her.

"Have we given each other the same gift? This is suspiciously similar, is it not?" And he chuckled again.

"It is indeed. Shall I open your gift to me?" she asked.

He nodded. He picked up the box and sat back, watching carefully as she undid the bow around her box.

She pulled out a pale green velvet hat and matching muff. Just right for the winter weather that was closing in around them. His mother had assured him this was the perfect style and fashion, and he knew the colour was Dianna.

"Oh, my dear, it is beautiful and very funny."

"Funny? Do you not like it?"

"I love it and the colour. It's beautiful. Please open your gift and you will understand."

He picked up the box and opened it. There inside the box was a riding hat. And in the shade of forest green. They had both thought of hats and the same colour.

They looked at each other and began to roar with laughter.

ENFIELD WATCHED them from his hiding place in the trees as they walked around the grounds. They looked happy and relaxed. It seemed to him they thought he would be deterred if they were here in the country. Then they were wrong. He knew he could make her happier once he had his way. She needed his strong arm. That was all. He was not yet prepared to give up. He wanted her virginity, and he was prepared to take it by force if she did not succumb to his charms. He was sure he could find her alone, eventually. A rake like Baird would go wandering eventually.

* * *

THE FOLLOWING days were a whirlwind of activity. Dianna was determined that Jason would see the estate and all its changes. She was proud of what she had achieved and wanted him to be proud of her. He would often make comments of praise to her. She in turn would take his hand or squeeze it or place her arms around him to express her joy. He was both enthusiastic and a fast learner. He took notes and made the point of telling her what he would change in his own estate with the knowledge he had gained.

She entered the library to find him at her desk making notes and points. She was wearing the dress made from the material he had given her two days ago. Her maid had spent the last two days with the help of others making the dress. She came in quietly wanting to surprise him. It was such a beautiful gift. She had given him home made honey that day, from the estate. He had been having it on toasted bread each morning.

Yesterday had been wine. His gift to her. He had said she was the fruit that made it so clear and beautiful to drink. She had given him handkerchiefs. She had embroidered his initials in them. He had one sticking out of his coat top pocket. She waited for him to lift his head.

With head down, he spoke, "My dearest, these are tremendous gains."

"Jason, how did you know it was me?"

He lifted his head. "Your perfume. You look wonderful in that dress. I knew that material would be so right for you."

"You did?"

"Well, after some pointers from my mother, yes. I wanted the material she helped me find it."

He came around from the back of her desk and took her into his arms.

"My love, these last few days only convinces me of your intelligence, your beauty and what an eye your father had. He saw you as you truly are, and I will be grateful to him forever. I am only sorry that I cannot tell him myself."

She held him in her arms and absorbed his aftershave. Sandalwood. The oil that always made her think of him. They stood there holding each other for what could have been hours.

"Excuse me, Aunt." She looked at Ada. She was unsure how long the girl had been in the room before she spoke, but she really did not care. She let Jason release her from his embrace.

"May I bring something to your attention, please?"

"But of course, Ada. What can I do for you?"

"I was riding with the groom this morning. I know that it's cold, but I love to ride. And it hasn't snowed yet. And do not worry. He was very careful at reminding me to ride both carefully and sensibly."

"I am pleased to hear it."

"Well, we both noticed an unusual man, a gentleman wandering down the road toward the village. We thought it strange as he was walking, it being such cold weather. As we rode by, he said hello. We both nodded at him but kept riding. Aunt, the man sent a shiver down my spine."

"Describe him to me, Ada." Jason's protective mannerisms had kicked in, she noticed.

She knew instinctively that he was thinking it was Enfield. They listened to her description. It sounded like him. She rang the bell and Jason asked the butler to send for the groom. A few minutes later he entered. Jason took charge. And she was happy for him to do so.

"Peter, are you able to describe the man you saw this morning?"

"Yes sir. He was tall. I would say slightly taller than you. He was a gentleman and had fine clothes. His hair was black and his eyes dark. I will not lie to you, sir. He gave me a weird feeling. As if he was a man with sinister motives."

Jason looked at her. "It's Enfield."

"But surely, he would not pursue me to my own estate? After all I have made it clear that I have no interest in the man."

"It makes no sense to me. I have written to him and told him to stay away." She grabbed his hand and gave it a squeeze.

"Did he reply to you?"

"No."

"Then I doubt he has any intention of heeding you."

"My dear, if you will allow me, I would like to call your servants and farming staff together to make them aware of the situation. I want him away from here, even if I have to escort him back to London myself."

"You need not ask, my dear. Peter, can you ask the butler to come to us?"

Peter turned and made his way out the door. She took Ada into her embrace. "Thank you for your wise observation. Do not fret. We will deal with this man."

* * *

TRUE TO HIS WORD, Jason discussed the situation with the staff and made it clear that they were to report to him as soon as "the man" was spotted.

Returning to the library, he sat quietly as he awaited tea to be brought in.

"I believe he will not get closer to the house. Everyone is on alert, and I am sure we can rid ourselves of him."

"I am not concerned. You will handle it. I just cannot understand why he is still around. Surely, he can see that my interest is only in you."

"He is a man who does not take no as an answer. And I know he despises me as much as I do him. I don't think he took kindly that we renewed our friendship when he began to show an interest in you."

He took her hand and kissed her fingers. "My darling. I would marry you tomorrow, but I do not think that wonderful event would rid us of this fiend. He is up to something. I just don't know what."

"Let us not think of him now. I have my gift to give you. Your parents arrive later this afternoon and I want to make sure you have your gift. We will be fully occupied once they are here."

* * *

SHE HANDED HIM THE PACKAGE. He could see that it was a book of some sort. But he opened it patiently. It was a beautifully bound leather book. He opened it but the pages were blank.

"I have noticed the large amounts of notes you have been taking while you have been here. I thought you could use this to place them in order and spend time thinking about them."

"Again, my darling, you surprise me. This is just what I would have asked for. I love it. Thank you. I will order my notes over the coming days."

He took her hand into his. "But I am awaiting my parent's arrival as they have the gift for today. In two days, it will be Christmas eve and I have still much that I would both give you and discuss with you."

The butler re-entered. "Ma'am. The Baird's have arrived."

DON'T TOUCH ME

joyous evening was had as the two families enjoyed dinner together. It had been some years since they had eaten together. Then Dianna's father had been alive. And her mother showed no sign of age or illness. Her brother and sister-in-law had also been alive. Now he watched as Ada became acquainted with them all. His own father was a frail man and not the tower of strength he had once been. He would watch over him carefully these coming days.

"And here, my boy, is the family bible that you requested I bring. I have done as you said." Lord Baird handed the great book to his son.

Jason placed the tome on the table in front of him. He opened it to the page he longed to see. There was his name and he hoped to place Dianna's next to it.

"I know you said you would give me your answer on Christmas day," he whispered in Dianna's ear. "But I hope you will allow me to make this my gift to you. A chance to become part of our family."

Dianna gazed at the page. She had a smile on her face, yet he could see a tear come to her eye.

"I do not believe that you will be disappointed."

That was what he had hoped to hear. Christmas may bring them both more joy than they had expected.

He looked at his father who had his hand on the top pocket of his jacket. That told him that his father had obtained the special licence for Dianna and him to marry on Christmas morning, if she agreed. And he would discuss that with her tomorrow.

* * *

Dianna opened the door to the stable and stepped in. Christmas was close. It was so exciting. She had agreed to have breakfast with Jason early so they could go for a walk and discuss their future. She was going to tell him she was ready to marry him. The stable was dark, and she was grateful for the light of the lamp she had brought with her. She made her way to the stall where her horse "Chester" was waiting for her. He greeted her with a whinny, and she nuzzled up against his beautiful tan nose.

"Now, that is a sight you don't see every day."

Dianna did not move or react. The voice was not one she expected to hear but did not want him to know that.

"What the hell are you doing in my stable, Enfield?"

"Now, now, my dear. Your language leaves a lot to be desired. A woman of your grace should not have such a fowl mouth."

He moved up behind her locking her between the stall and himself, his arms on either side of her. She was no desperate innocent and could feel quite clearly his erection being pushed into her back.

She pushed back, knocking him slightly off balance but not enough for her to get away. All it allowed her was the moment to turn and face the demon.

"You had better leave now. You do not know me. You have no right to be here."

"I have no intention of going anywhere. You have rejected me for the last time. I will know you, in all senses of the word. Do you understand?"

"What on earth are you raving about? I have never given you any opportunity to get close to me. I despise you and have indicated that at every opportunity."

"Playing hard to get makes no difference to me. I intend to have both of you."

"What in heavens name can you mean?"

It was then she heard the muffled cries of Ada.

She looked from side to side and over to her right she saw the bound body of her niece.

"If you have laid a hand on her, I swear I will kill you with my own hands."

"Now, now. She is intact, for now. I thought that I would have her in front of you. After all you are both virgins. And I will delight in having you both."

She started pounding him in the chest.

"Jason will be meeting me here any minute. He will tear you limb from limb."

"I am no fool, madam. He has been taken care of. You see, I made passionate love to one of your maids. And she would do anything for me. Place poison in his brandy glass, for example. You know the one he had before he said his goodnight to you and went to bed? He should be dying in agony and all alone, about now."

Dianna pictured the glass she had seen in Jason's hand. She had seen it. It was empty. He had drunk it before he wished her a wonderful night's sleep. Her head dropped.

"Ah, then you saw him drink the brew."

"No. I did not. I just saw him holding the empty glass." She wanted to cry. Both in anger and disgust.

"That is enough for me. Baird is dying and I plan to have sex with you and the fair young maiden on the floor. You see, I do not trust you. I assume you have already laid down with Baird. So, I need to wipe your memory of him. You will know only my touch before you die."

She began to beat him on his chest again. "I love Jason not you."

He took his hand and slapped her hard around her face.

"You bastard," she cried.

"Trust me, my dear. I can make this very difficult and painful for you, and your niece. As you have not denied being with Jason then I will have you first and finish with the virgin."

"Bastard."

He began by grabbing her hands and with one hand he held her hands behind her back. With his other hand he slapped her across her face again.

"I will not be silent."

"Shut your mouth or I will break your neck and still take you."

"I will not shut up. You, sir, are despicable. Someone will come. Someone will hear."

"I would agree with that." Came the voice of her beloved Jason. He did not appear ill, and he certainly was not dead.

In one fast movement, Enfield swung her around and threw her toward Ada on the ground. He held a knife in his hand and was pointing it at Jason.

"What may I ask, do you plan to do with that?" Jason questioned as he pointed to the knife.

"Quite simple, Baird. I plan to kill you and then have my way with the two women on the floor."

"I don't think so."

"And why do you think that, fool?"

"Because you, sir, underestimate my Dianna. And yes, she is my Dianna. She will never be yours." He stood there with crossed arms as if he had not a care in the world.

With that Dianna, using the hammer from the wall near Ada, swung at Enfield's head, hearing, and feeling the deadening thump as she hit him. Enfield was on the floor and blood was pouring from the wound on his head.

"How dare he?" She dropped the hammer and ran back to Ada to untie the poor girl.

Jason leaned down to see if the villain was still alive. He was. But he was going to have a terrible headache. Two manservants came in with the maid she assumed Enfield had hoodwinked. The poor silly girl screamed and ran to his side.

Dianna then blurted her immediate concern as she loosened the last of the twine that bound Ada. "He had poisoned your brandy. We must try to save you." She ran and threw herself into Jason's arms.

"You need not fear, my dear. I did not drink it. I noticed the smell of almonds as I took in the aroma of the brandy. I placed the contents in a nearby plant. At least then whoever was waiting to see an empty glass would assume, I had drunk the concoction. I have smelt cyanide before. I then spoke to the servants and the maid soon revealed her error, confessing all."

She held him close. Not letting him go. She caught her breath on a smile, he was clearly a clever man. And he was willing to come and protect her from a man who would try to hurt Ada as well as her. Enfield was stronger than her but not as intelligent. Jason's words came to her again.

"You underestimate my Dianna."

"You allowed me to hit him." She was puzzled.

"If I had hit him, I would have killed him. Believe me, I could not have stopped myself. Besides, you needed to stop him to protect your niece. I was here only if you needed help. You did not. Besides, it will be interesting for all to know that he was bested by a woman. And my dear, what a woman."

She hugged him all the harder. He would allow her to be herself and still protect her. She loved him all the more.

Despite Enfield's attempts to hurt them, a doctor was called for and he was taken to one of the rooms in the stable to await his arrival. She would treat him better than he had planned to treat her. The magistrate was called and informed, and they left it in his hands to deal with him.

* * *

Dianna appeared to be calm, but he sensed she was more disturbed with what had nearly happened than she was allowing anyone to see. Poor Ada was cold and in tears. More brandy was fetched and checked to be free of any impurities or poisons. Ada was given a small amount to warm her. She was wrapped in a rug and had her head resting on her aunt's lap.

"He did nothing to hurt you?" Dianna's concern for her niece was evident.

"No, Aunt. I have bruises and alike from trying to fight him off, but he tied me up and then waited for you. I kicked him and struggled as much as I could. I fought him as you did."

She had stopped crying and had taken on a fierce anger toward Enfield. He could not blame her for that. The young girl had more strength than most girls her age but then she was Dianna's niece.

"It would seem she has the same fighting spirit as her aunt." He handed a glass of brandy to Dianna. She drank nearly all of it in one gulp and looked at him, handed him the glass which he refilled and handed back to her.

The parents were soon in the library with them ascertaining to their wellbeing. They fussed, having tea brought in and more blankets were duly wrapped around the young ladies. The magistrate arrived and asked them what had happened and about Jason's arrival at the stable. The magistrate was angry that Jason had hit him so hard and said so.

Dianna stood up and came to stand before the magistrate.

"I assure you, sir, that it was I, who hit him with the hammer. He was about to do despicable things to me and my niece."

"My aunt was protecting me." Ada insisted from the chaise.

"Well, Enfield says that you sir, hit him." He was looking at Jason.

Jason laughed out loud.

"Mr Fitzsimons, he is loathsome. He doesn't want it to be known that a woman had the better of him."

Dianna stood there with her hands on her hips. "I can assure you it was I."

Jason smiled. "I'd agree with that. Believe me, I would love to claim the credit, but I cannot. She was like a mother cat protecting her kittens. And Enfield got scratched."

Mr Fitzsimons began to laugh. "I have known you all your life Dianna. I have seen your temper. I believe you and respect your place in protecting yourself and your niece. Leave it with me." He turned and left.

The family stayed with them a while. Jason did all that he could to have their fears relieved and eventually sent them back to bed. Soon it was just she and Ada, and he left in the room.

"Aunt, can I stay in your room tonight?" she asked timidly.

The poor girl was exhausted. And although shaken was looking for some reassurance.

"Of course, my dear. Now you head up to my room and I will be with you shortly."

Ada gingerly got up with the blanket still wrapped around her. "I may have a bath. I am somewhat soiled after being in the stables half the night."

"Do my dear and take your time." Dianna watched her go. As soon as the doors were closed, she sighed and began to weep. No hysterics, just weeping. The emotions had gotten the better of her.

He came and sat next to her and lifted her onto his lap and just held her as she cried. And she did cry. After about ten minutes she had stopped weeping and was just holding on to him.

That was when he spoke.

"Marry me, my darling Dianna. Allow me to protect you with my name and my body. I am aware that you can take care of yourself, but I have grown so much in love with you. Perhaps we can go forward together?" He drew her in closer.

"I will marry you but not for your protection but because I cannot imagine you not being by my side from this day forward."

"Thank you. But you will have my protection and my love. And I love you with every part of my being."

He continued to hold her. No more words were needed.

CHRISTMAS IS COMING

The few days before Christmas day were somewhat of a whirlwind. Plans were made for a Christmas day wedding. The special licence was taken to their local church and the ceremony was to be an addition to the Christmas day service. This would allow her estate friends as well as the families to rejoice in the joy she was now feeling.

"Ada is so excited that she will be maid of honour."

"And she was just like you when your brother married. Fourteen, excited and on the verge of new experiences."

"I am just annoyed that Enfield has spoilt the last of our twelve days of gift giving."

"I am not, as my greatest gift will be that we are finally united. Besides, we still have the gifts, and we can open them after we are married. Now I plan to enjoy a special day with you. Our wedding day. And you are the greatest gift you could ever give to me."

"So, I will say goodnight and see you at the church in the morning."

"Sleep well, my dear, as tomorrow you will be sleeping in my arms for ever more."

* * *

"You look beautiful, Diamond." The carriage was gently rocking. It slowly went out the gate of the estate.

"That cream lace goes so well with your hair, Aunt. And to have some of your hair up and the rest flowing around your neck, you are captivating. And the hood, fur lined is Christmas."

"Why, thank you Ada. That is wonderful of you to say." She took her hand. "I am so proud of you. You have not allowed that horrible Enfield to hurt your spirit. You are a talented and strong young lady."

"Ahh, that is because I have an aunt who has shown me to love who you love and tell those who treat you badly to get out of the way. And use a hammer if they don't listen." She laughed merrily. "If you do not mind me saying, Aunt, Jason is a man to be proud of. A man who loves you for all the right reasons."

"Ada, I do believe you are right."

The three ladies held hands as the carriage came to a stop outside the church. First her niece came down the stairs and walked over to the entrance of the church. Her mother took her hands into hers.

"I am so very proud of you and of Jason. He is a special man. Not many would come to help the women they love to run their estate. You are a very lucky woman."

"Yes Mother, I believe that I am."

"And he is a lucky man. He has a diamond."

Her mother descended the carriage and made her way into the church. She had a definite bounce in her steps.

The lace of her dress was soft and flowing as she descended the coach. The woollen cream and fur muffs wrapped around her hands made the warmth travel through her body. The cream overcoat that was also fur lined, and hood allowed her to be warm but still very much the bride.

She made her way to the end of the aisle and looked up at the man who was waiting at the altar to marry her. With pride and pleasure, she made her way up the aisle as a harp played Mozart. Her father was not there to give her away. So, she walked confidently forward with Ada just ahead of her. She wanted to marry Jason and was happy to show the world she gave herself to him.

He was dressed as any gentleman would and wore the cream vest to match her lace dress. A dress she had not worn because it was too beautiful to wear for day and needed a special occasion. That occasion had arrived. They looked into each other's eyes as the priest began to speak. But it was just them. Though others were there she only had eyes for Jason.

* * *

THEY WERE to travel to his father's estate after a few days to have a break from the excitement of the past few weeks and the glorious wedding. He was contemplating this as he awaited his wife's entrance to their bedroom. His wife. That sounded so delightful. Yet only a few short weeks ago marriage was further from his mind than it ever had been. Then he met his Dianna again. She would be the partridge in his family tree. He chuckled to himself.

As if on cue she came in from the dressing room. She had changed out of her beautiful cream lace wedding dress into a beautiful lace and cotton night dress. It gathered under her breast and showed her figure to perfection. She stepped over the fireplace, allowing the light from the fire to silhouette her figure. She was magnificent. He stood and came over to her and took her into his arms.

"My love, you are exquisite." He held her close. "I wish to give you the last of the twelve gifts. They are important to me. Before I make love to you, you need to know."

"Very well." She smiled at him.

"Do not be disappointed, my dear. It will lead on to I hope a very wonderful and pleasurable evening."

He watched as her blush rose to her cheeks.

"Day ten should have been this." And he handed her a small flat box, unwrapped. She took it and opened it to find four sapphires shining on a necklace. He took it from the box and fastened it around her neck. She went over to the mirror to see her reflection.

"Oh Jason, it is truly beautiful. Thank you." She went to the mantle to get her gift to him.

"I had this made especially as I had every intention of saying yes, I will marry you." She opened a box and pulled out something that gave a quick glint of gold. She placed it in the palm of his hand. It was a ring. It had a great black stone in it. But in the stone stood his and her initials carved into it.

"My wedding ring, you could say. I will wear this knowing that you wanted to marry me even before I asked again. Thank you." He took her in his arms for a moment.

"Day eleven was to be this." He went to the table beside the bed and brought over a document. "These state clearly that though we are married you retain all of your inheritance. That it remains yours to pass on to whomever you desire. As your husband, I know that what is yours is mine, but I make no claim on it. I have signed it, as you see."

He watched her for her reaction. She smiled at him.

"We can share it. But I would like Ada to have some of the estate when she is of age. Until then you and I can keep it safe for her." She hugged him again and he held her, just feeling their hearts beating.

She looked up at him. "I need to confess that I had not come up with an idea for day eleven as the ring was to say you will now have me."

"Well, that is the best gift of all. We have each other."

"And for day twelve we have given each other to each other."

"Ah, yes my dear." He lifted her up and took her to the bed. "But that is the best gift of all. I will love you all my life. Come let me show you."

ABOUT THE AUTHOR

Joanne loves to write and she loves to travel. She is married to Andrew and lives in Central New South Wales Australia with him and their two cats Arthur and Oscar. (Meet them on Joanne's webpage) She has two grown sons and four beautiful granddaughters. Her imagination loves to take her on various trips but mainly in the area of the regency romance.

She also loves meeting new people so do drop a line to her on:

Website Facebook Instagram Twitter

I have loved using folk law and traditional history in this series. It has spurred my imagination. I love the way the fae have developed in the story and that they too are not perfect and can give a few bad apples to history.

Having mixed marriages was an idea which was there from the beginning but the fae blood would only appear in the females. That too was my idea and I loved playing with it. If you have loved this story, then you will definitely not want to miss the final in the series "Glenna's Future". And please tell your friends about this series.

Keep a look out for it. It will appear later this year.

And just to tempt you here is the cover...

Go to my website and subscribe to my newsletter. It is only monthly so you won't be bombarded by emails.

https://www.joanneaustenbrown.com/

or join me on my Facebook page.

https://www.facebook.com/joanne.boog/

MORE BOOKS BY JOANNE AUSTEN BROWN

Always Louisa (Always Series Book 1)

Louisa Stapleton has been disgraced and banished from society. She wants to return to defend herself and seize the life she desires. Her father has obtained the help of the one man she sees as her nemesis. Arriving at the house party, she has her doubts about her success in returning.

Chalanor Farraday, the Viscount Lightford, had a hand in her downfall but he was not a willing participant. To redeem his honour he wants to help her back into the society that rejected her. But she hates him. That is the last thing he wants. Can he convince her to trust him?

Can they overcome the trials that they will face so that Louisa can obtain more than she had hoped for? Neither see the figures lurking in the shadows. They want to prevent her return to society. And they have their reasons for wanting her dead. Will they succeed?

Rachael's Jaunt (Come With Me Book 1)

Rachael Fielding loves Scotland. She escapes her busy life for some down time but does not expect that time to be in 1822. Is she dreaming? And why is the man she knows as her dream Scotsman suddenly there in front of her?

Duncan Murray is a laird though he does not want to be. But he was born to the position. Then Rachael shows up and his world is turned upside down. Can she be the love of his life and what have the Fae got to do with it?

Is she a spy for the soon to visit, King George 4th? Can he believe her stories of the future? The two will be tested to their limits. Will the Fae have their way and is there a future for Duncan and Rachael?

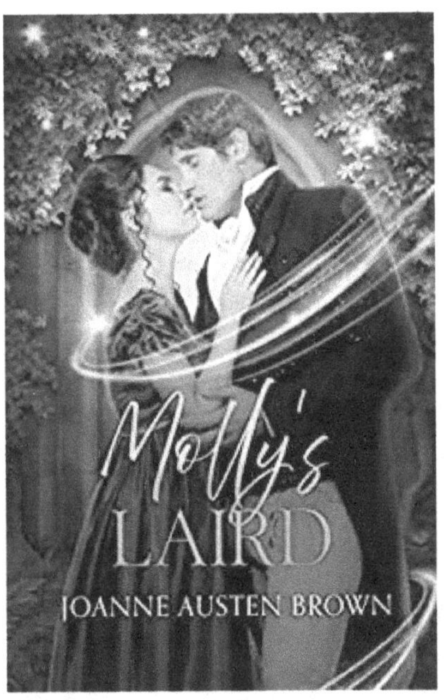

Molly's Laird (Come With Me)

In her own time Molly is a fish out of water. But when she goes back in time to find some peace, after the deaths of all her family, she finds a new beginning.

Can all the promises of the past be true? What about the Fae? And can this handsome man be just for her?

Alasdair misses his brother but understands why he left. He is now Laird but is lonely. Will he find love like Duncan did? Who is the real Molly he cannot stop thinking of? Is she the answer to all he has been searching for? What are the Fae up to?

Always
Delia
JOANNE AUSTEN BROWN

Glenna's
FUTURE
JOANNE AUSTEN BROWN